BIG TRACTOR

Nathan Clement

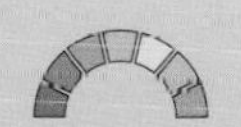

BOYDS MILLS PRESS
AN IMPRINT OF HIGHLIGHTS
Honesdale, Pennsylvania

Thanks to John and Ronda Jones for sharing your farm equipment, time, and your friendship down through the years.

Thanks to Terome Gough for your expert farmer's eye.

Boyds Mills Press, Inc.
An Imprint of Highlights
815 Church Street
Honesdale, Pennsylvania 18431
Printed in China
ISBN: 978-1-62091-790-9
Library of Congress Control Number: 2014943970
First edition

The text for this book is set in Calvert MT.

The pictures in this book are computer-rendered. Just as an artist may use oil paint, Nathan uses color fills and blends within shapes to create his artwork. Every picture he makes begins as a pencil drawing before the computer magic can ever happen.

10 9 8 7 6 5 4 3

To Ardelia Williams—thank you for your decades of dedication to Indiana Wesleyan University art students.

Wake up, Ol' Partner.
It's springtime!

Time to hitch up the plow.
Time to turn up the soil.

Get along, Ol' Partner.
Run the disc and smooth the dirt.

Hurry up!
Time to tow the planter.
Time to seed the rows.

Have a rest, Ol' Partner.
Let's watch the crops grow.

Get a move on!
It's summertime.

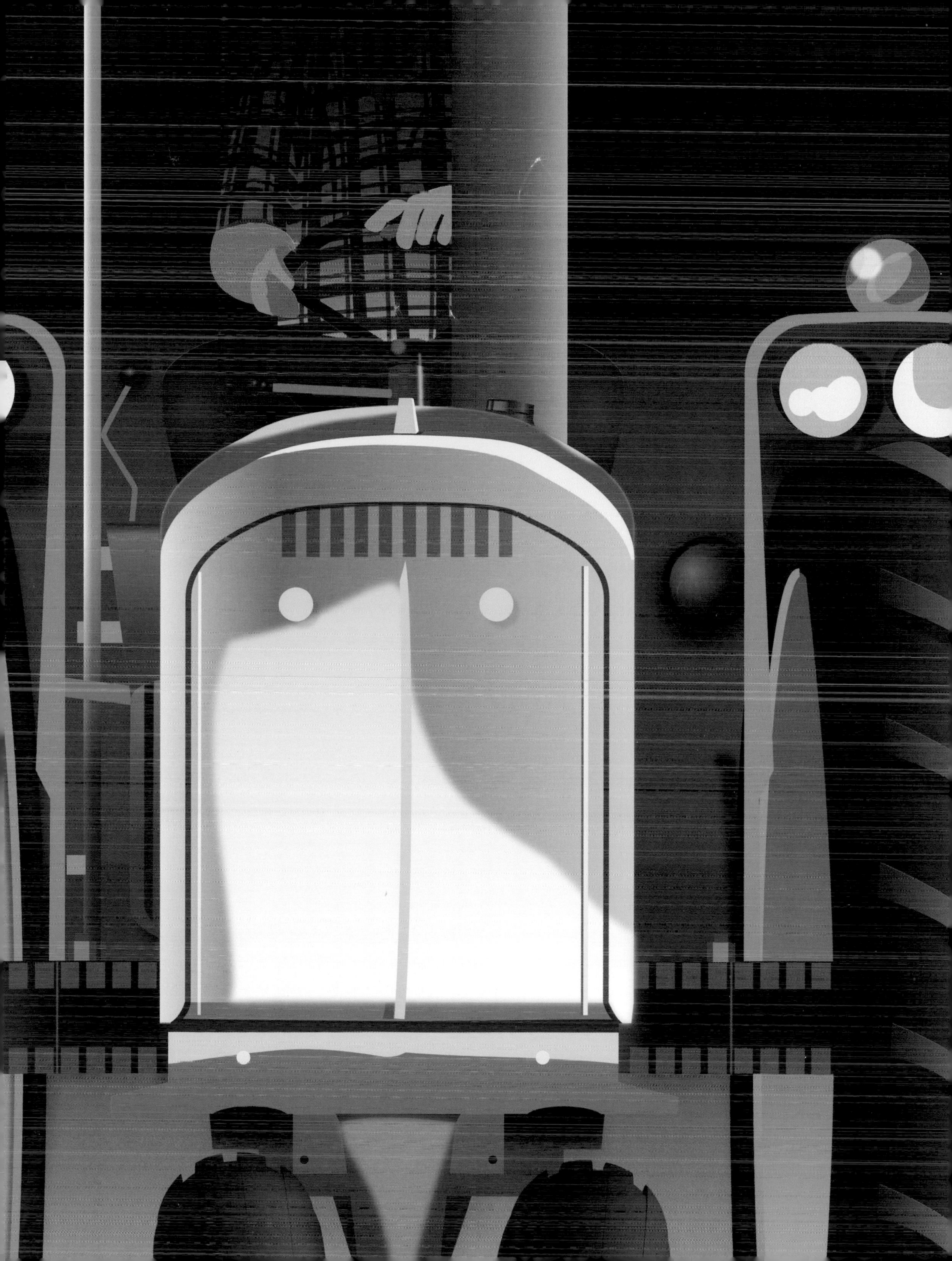

Time to hook up the mower.
Time to cut down the clover.

Back it up, Ol' Partner.
We'll run the elevator to fill the haymow.

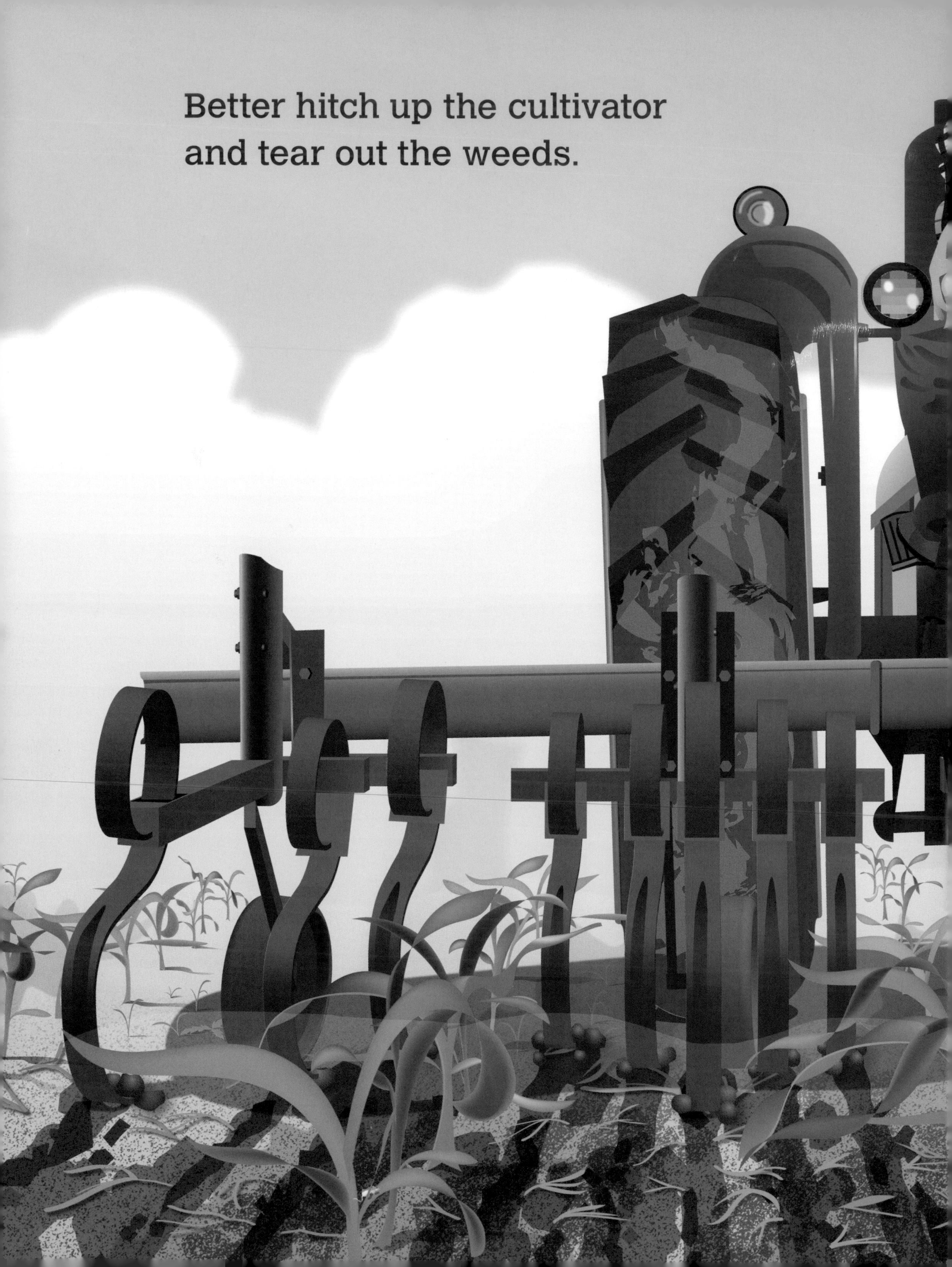

Better hitch up the cultivator
and tear out the weeds.

Take a break, Ol' Partner.
Time to start up the combine.
Time to cut down the wheat.

Back to work, Ol' Partner.
It's autumn harvest time.

Time to pull the grain wagon.
Time to haul in the corn.

Now it's time to have some fun.